Words to Know Before You Read

boss

crawling

enough

freeze

make

play

rules

together

www.rourkeeducationalmedia.com

Edited by Precious McKenzie
Illustrated by Anita DuFalla
Art Direction and Page Layout by Renee Brady

To Dr. Jean, Cheryl, and Valerie- thank you for inspiring me, mentoring me, and being my friend. - Sam

Library of Congress PCN Data

I'm the Boss! / Sam Williams
ISBN 978-1-61810-164-8 (hard cover) (alk. paper)
ISBN 978-1-61810-297-3 (soft cover)
Library of Congress Control Number: 2012936765

Rourke Educational Media
Printed in China, Artwood Press Limited,
  Shenzhen, China

rourkeeducationalmedia.com

customerservice@rourkeeducationalmedia.com • PO Box 643328 Vero Beach, Florida 32964

I'm the Boss!

By Sam Williams

Illustrated by Anita DuFalla

"Let's go play!"

4

C'mon everyone!

"I'm the boss. I make the rules."

"We're going to play freeze tag!"

"Can I play?"

"You're not fast enough."

"Let him play."

"No one wants to play
with a crawling cub."

"Abby Gator, you're NOT the boss."

After Reading Activities

You and the Story...

Who was being a bully?

What did she do?

How did Cooper Cub resolve the problem?

Words You Know Now...

Can you make a sentence using two of the words below?
Can you make a sentence using three of these words?

boss   make
crawling   play
enough   rules
freeze   together

You Could...Make Up A New Game

- What will you call your game?

- How many people can play your game?

- What are the rules for your game?

- How do you win your new game?

- Invite some friends to play your new game.

About the Author

Sam lives with his two dogs, Abby and Cooper, in Florida. Abby and Cooper often play games with each other...their favorite game is chase.

Ask The Author!
www.rem4students.com

About the Illustrator

Acclaimed for its versatility in style, Anita DuFalla's work has appeared in many educational books, newspaper articles, and business advertisements and on numerous posters, book and magazine covers, and even giftwraps. Anita's passion for pattern is evident in both her artwork and her collection of 400 patterned tights. She lives in the Friendship neighborhood of Pittsburgh, Pennsylvania with her son, Lucas.